Jack In Dreamschool

About the author

Ruth Beech currently lives in a village in Cambridgeshire with her husband, two teenaged sons, and Jack Russell dog. She has been studying Traditional Chinese Medicine practices since 2001, Tibetan Buddhism since 2002, and teaching qi gong, meditation and acupressure massage since 2003. Prior to this, her degree in Philosophy with History of Art, and then her Master of Science in Educational Research all indicate her wide range of interests and experiences. Since her sons were young, Ruth has learned a lot about neurodiversity through observation, courses, and reading. Her MSc dissertation focussed on whether children who are happy in school achieve more positive outcomes. Looking into the happiness of children in a school setting turned out to be very relevant for her life as a parent to two autistic children who were very unhappy in mainstream school.

Jack In Dreamschool

Sometimes Dreams Make More Sense than Real Life

Written and illustrated by
Ruth Beech

Published by Mischmasch Publishing

First published 2024

Front cover artwork and design by Ruth Beech
Cover layout designed by Deborah Ripley

For Mani and Jobi

I am in your heart wherever you go,
as you are in mine wherever I am.
You don't need to be scared of anything
Or anyone, I am in your heart.
You have more than enough love and strength
To face whatever comes your way.
It's your own heart, your own strength,
But with an extra layer of comfort and capacity.
If you ever need me, I am in your heart.

Love, Mum

Table of Contents

Problems at Home

Jack woke up with a sense of dread that filled his whole body, radiating out from his belly as if little caterpillars were crawling around inside. This was not a new feeling and it wasn't particular to this day. It was, after all, a school day. He lay in his bed hoping it might really be Sunday morning, but could hear his brother clattering around as he went out of the front door to college. A few moments later, Jack's mum gently knocked on his door and popped her head around it. He pretended he was still asleep, so she left him to get up when he was ready, leaving the door open to let in some light, in the hope that would help to wake him up.

This is one of the little habits Jack's mum had developed over the years from realising that Jack does a lot better when he can be allowed to do things in his own time, and in his own way. Getting cross and shouting at Jack to hurry up and so on just makes him feel really sad and anxious. It also made his mum and dad feel the same way. There had been some mornings when Jack was very young when his mum had got really frustrated that he still hadn't got dressed even by the time they should be leaving the house.

She had started reading books about the best ways to parent children who 'blew up' easily and she sought help very early on, when Jack was only a year or two old, when the usual parenting techniques just made things worse. It was hard to understand why life just seemed so very difficult for Jack, even though at home he was full of love and laughter. You see, Jack found it very hard to put into words why he froze in certain situations, or got so embarrassed when he was hurt, and why he reacted so angrily when he was told what to do.

When he was a toddler, Jack's mum and dad tried everything they could to teach Jack not to touch plug sockets and bins, but he really didn't seem to be able to stop himself. He was very different from his brother, who was autistic and had a very clear sense of what was allowed and what was not. So, it really didn't make sense when Jack's mum sought support from schools or professionals and they remarked things like "he's just copying his brother". *But he's nothing like his brother! The only thing Jack might have in common with his brother is that he is also autistic.*

PDA was one of those terms that people seem to have never heard of until they need to find out why their child finds it so hard to follow instructions or just get on with what's asked of them. It stands for 'pathological demand avoidance', or maybe more accurately, a 'pervasive desire for autonomy'. As soon as Jack's mum read about this distinct part of the autistic spectrum, everything started to fall into place. Far from the standard way of viewing disruptive children, it was not the case at all that Jack was finding things really difficult and overwhelming on purpose, of course he wasn't! It was just that Jack's brain's natural response is to feel anxious any time something feels like a demand, and to him **everything** feels like a demand. Jack had become so much more relaxed and happy at home since his mum and dad stopped telling him what to do directly, and no longer misunderstood his distressed responses. It was such a different way of thinking about parenting that his dad took a bit longer to get his head around it, and some other family members were still catching up. Parenting a PDA child is hard, especially when all the support that's around for 'challenging behaviour' when they're young has no understanding of PDA.

At home, when there were things that needed to get done (like leaving the house, or brushing teeth) Jack's mum and dad had learned that asking Jack how he felt about doing these everyday things, and when he thought he would be able to do them, and giving him **lots** of advance notice about anything that was happening, meant he wasn't reacting so anxiously. One hurdle that still felt insurmountable, however, was going to school. Before he could even leave the house for school in the morning, getting dressed in his uncomfortable uniform was the biggest ordeal for Jack. "How am I supposed to focus in class when this feels so annoying!?" Jack mumbled crossly to himself. "Are you okay?" his mum asked from behind the door. She seemed to be the only person who understood he really was not doing this on purpose; he just couldn't wear most clothes because they were too uncomfortable.

"Fine. Just these stupid clothes!" Jack said quietly, feeling stressed and that he didn't really know quite how to put his intense distress and discomfort into words. He knew his mum believed him, he had heard her explaining to his dad that clothes appeared to actually hurt him, but Jack still felt the pressure of having to wear school clothes. After all, that's what was expected, it is what everyone has to do, as he had been told repeatedly. For a few years now Jack's head teachers had said it was okay for him to wear the soft t-shirts to school that his mum had spent a long time through trial and error finding for him, but now he was in secondary school there were some teachers who didn't seem to have got the memo. They repeatedly told Jack off in front of his friends and embarrassed him for being different. It was very tiring having to force himself to put on an act every day for school, hiding his discomfort so people didn't think he was strange. In fact, by Tuesday afternoons he was always exhausted, and his mum would sometimes ask if he was feeling unwell because of how grey his face looked.

"I'm fine." was usually his stock response so that the attention would be turned away from him quickly.

Jack knew that he was tired, but didn't really know why. He had managed to develop a decent sleep routine now that his mum and dad had let him be in charge of it, and waking up a few times most nights, worrying about this and that, was something he was used to. The weariness was only there during the school week.

That Monday at school passed like every other - slowly and painfully. The only thing that gave Jack comfort was playtimes with his friends. When his mum picked Jack up from school in the car that rainy day and asked him what he had done that had been fun, his flat response of "Nothing." let her know there probably wasn't much point trying to find out about his day until later. *At least he made it in* she thought to herself, remembering the many Mondays when he had just been too stressed about school and getting dressed to leave the house. There had been many times during Jack's final year at primary school when he had been late getting there in the morning. The headteacher had tried to be understanding, but it was clear they thought Jack's mum was just not trying hard enough and needed to be more in control. "Tell him you'll have to drive him to school in his pyjamas if he won't get dressed." Fortunately, Jack's mum had told Jack this as a joke rather than making him feel like he had done something wrong, knowing how much he was struggling. It helped so much when Jack was helped to see the funny side of things.

That night, before pulling his blind down, Jack stood in his room looking out at the brightly lit window of a house that faces his bedroom. It's quite a distance away, so when you glance out at it, it resembles a rectangular moon. He put his ear buds in his ears, and turned on his audiobook to drown out the anxious thoughts that clutter his brain. After a few minutes of just standing, watching and listening, Jack pulled the blind down, straightened the pens and pencils on his desk, and climbed into bed. His audiobook was set to turn off in 40 minutes; he always sets the timer to make sure it goes off after he's fallen asleep, that way he can focus on what he's listening to instead of his worries. This usually works quite well, but thoughts about school keep Jack awake. *Secondary school is so much harder than primary, and that was bad enough. There's not enough time between lessons for me to get used to what's just gone on, or to get ready for what the next teacher's mood might be like.* He turned up the volume on his phone so the audiobook was louder than his thoughts, and eventually fell asleep.

****

The next morning was much the same as the day before, and all of Jack's previous school days. After some squeals of discomfort and already feeling weary after the ordeal of getting dressed and ready for school, Jack came downstairs, put the harness on his dog, Diddly, and gave him a stroke while waiting to set off with his mum. They walked along talking about this and that, crossed the small green next to their house then turned the corner to join the rest of the families making their way up and down the village high street, some going towards Jack's old primary school, and the rest going towards Jack's secondary school. Jack and his mum came up to where Jack meets his friend Martin to walk the rest of the way to school. Jack's mum asked him "Did you enjoy the special assembly yesterday?" He took a while to answer but his mum was used to this and so gave him a few moments, before checking he had heard.

"Not really. I didn't remember until I got to class that it was happening, and they made us sit in different places." Jack's mum felt a little bit sad as he said this; she remembered seeing how uncomfortable he looked when she had gone into his assembly years ago when Jack was 'star of the week'. She could still picture him in that big hall now, looking lost and anxious because he didn't have space around him to move. A couple of the other children had been unknowingly leaning or brushing against him. After his mum had explained to his teacher that Jack didn't cope very well with people being so close to him, Jack

had been allowed to stay at the back of the line so that he was at the end of a row, with plenty of space.
That was a few years ago, however, and she had no idea whether that need had been long forgotten now he was in a much busier secondary school.

Trying to brighten his mood, she asked "Was it okay though?"
"Yeah, some of it but I can't really remember what it was about." Jack always noticed everything around him and got distracted by any movements or noises, so it was never easy to follow what he was meant to be focusing on at his hectic school. He loved spending time with his friends and was well liked because he was so fun to be around. Although he often called out or did other unexpected things in class, teachers tended to just see him as 'cheeky' in the lower years of primary school and so he didn't get into much trouble. Now he was getting older, however, and the distractedness was obviously not going away. His teachers, and some classmates, became increasingly exasperated by Jack's unpredictable behaviour. Teachers no longer found it endearing that he impulsively said random things and even went up and drew on the whiteboard when he was bored. The work that the teachers had to set was getting harder and there was more and more content to fit into lessons. There were so many children to try to teach and maintain the attention of. Of course,

Jack found some teachers more interesting or understanding than others. For many of the teachers, any children who couldn't just sit still and be quiet were a pain, and they often did not mind letting them know.

When his mum was occasionally asked for suggestions to help Jack focus for longer periods, his mum's ideas were treated with suspicion at best, and completely ignored at worst. The teachers were usually nice enough, but Jack's mum was often left with the feeling that they just did not really have time to worry about making school a nicer place to be. After all, they had to keep up with all their paperwork, and "Jack isn't the only child in the class that has issues."

"Do try to work with the school," was a line she sometimes heard, but at the same time it seemed that they weren't interested in working with Jack's mum or seeing her as an ally and willing to listen to what was working at home.

So, every day was a struggle for Jack, starting on Sundays, when he began to dread the school week ahead.

Fine at School

Nonetheless, they met up with Martin, and Jack's mum waved him off to school like every other day (she often felt it was a miracle they had got there on time after the way the morning had gone), and like every other day, Jack found it very hard to let his mum leave. At least he didn't still cling onto her arm and cry in desperation as the teaching assistant prised him off her like the early years of primary school.
"He'll be fine once he can't see you anymore!" the teaching assistant would always say, sometimes chirpily, sometimes crossly. Strange that they continued to think that despite Jack doing this every day for about three years since starting reception. Now, Jack dealt with the anxiety of leaving his mum by asking her questions that she was sure he already knew the answer to, until eventually it got so late that Martin told Jack they needed to get going quickly, and would start rushing off for school. Jack gave Diddly's head a ruffle, said "Bye" to his mum, and rushed off after Martin. The two boys hurried along the street to their secondary school, trying along with the rest of the pupils to not be the last ones through the gates as the teacher waiting there shooed them in.

"Jack, sit down! Everyone else is ready." Mr Brown boomed across the classroom as Jack entered a few moments after Martin. Jack's heart raced as he panicked and his cheeks flushed. He didn't look around because he was so embarrassed already and knew everyone would be looking. It was only 8:50am and Jack was already thoroughly exhausted. He quickly sat in his seat, and put his head down on his folded arms on his desk, trying to make himself as small as possible.

****

"Woof, woof!" Jack suddenly looked up to see if Diddly really was there in his classroom. Looking round, he realised there were just a handful of other children in the class with him, and they didn't seem to have heard a dog barking - Diddly wasn't there, of course! Also, it wasn't only Mr Brown and the part time teaching assistant in the room, but also another adult. Although Jack didn't remember who they were, he instantly felt at ease with her being there as well. In fact, he felt much more relaxed than usual in every way. This was such a strange occurrence in school that he took a few moments to look around and try to work out what was causing this unexpected sense of calm. The first thing he noticed was that the lights in the classroom were less bright, and they were slowly changing from one colour to another. It was daytime outside, of course, so these colours must be coming from a lamp, he realised.
Jack stood up, tentatively at first because Mr Brown usually told him off for walking round the room, but Mr Brown looked over and simply smiled at him and gave an encouraging little nod. Surprised, but delighted, Jack walked over to the corner of the room where he had spotted the colour changing lamp. Not only was the remote control for the lamp just left there for anyone to use, but there were also a couple of comfortable cushioned armchairs, and a whole box of fiddle toys. There was also the softest rug that Jack had ever touched - and he absolutely had to touch it, just to see if it was as soft as it looked!

"Are you okay, Jack?"
Jack had a little panic at Mr Brown's question, but then realised that he was smiling and had asked in a rather throw away fashion, not demanding or cross at all.
"Yes, thank you, Sir," He ventured. "I was just looking at the light."
"I know it took a while for us to get it, but it was a great suggestion you had. It's so soothing, isn't it."
"Yes, Sir." Jack responded, trying not to sound too confused. He couldn't remember suggesting they get colour changing lights, but knowing how much it helps him feel calm at home, it did seem like something he would have suggested if given the chance. Well, maybe his memory wasn't as brilliant as his parents always told him it was. Jack decided to just go with it, as Mr Brown seemed to be in such a good mood. He smiled to himself and played with the remote control to see what else it could do with the colour patterns and brightness. Just then, Jack's friend Martin came over and plonked himself down in one of the comfy seats with a book. He didn't speak to Jack, but they had been friends since pre-school and there was a kind of quiet bond between them. "This is really good, isn't it?" Jack whispered.
"What? Yeah." Martin said back, shaking his head at his friend's typically odd comment, and getting back to reading his book.

Jack looked around again, taking everything in. *It certainly looks like my classroom…I think. But it feels different,* Jack thought to himself. He noticed again how calm he was feeling, with none of the racing thoughts and heartbeat that usually followed him through his days at school. *What* is *different then?* Jack looked across the room and noticed that the tables were more spaced out and there were only two chairs to most tables, and just one on some. There were two tables at the edge of the room that had side partitions between them like the ones in a call centre. He had thought the rest of his classmates must be out doing something else that he hadn't realised or remembered was happening today, but now it seemed clear that there were actually only spaces for eight children in the class altogether. Was this a new arrangement his mum had received a letter about and not passed on? She knows how he needs to be kept informed of what's happening ahead of time and in as much detail as possible so that he can process it and picture how it might look, sound and feel. Jack's school teachers didn't seem to understand this about him, as they were always springing changes to the day on the children without warning. Jack assumed he wasn't the only one of his classmates who didn't like not knowing what was going on.

But that must be what had happened. Although, this change wasn't making Jack panic at all. Instead,

he was feeling much more relaxed than he could remember feeling before at school. He had already noticed that Mr Brown seemed to be in a very good mood, and none of the teachers were giving him annoyed glances, or telling him to stop doing something he hadn't even realised he was doing. It didn't seem like Martin noticed anything different as he was just reading his book as though this is where he always did so.
But I'm sure this is the first time Martin has ever looked so relaxed in class. He's usually sat bolt upright at our desk, looking nervous whenever the teachers look over or start talking.
Jack had grasped, rather guiltily, that Martin was often nervous because Jack was making some sort of noise or fidgeting. He was hesitant, but wanted to ask Martin a question just to check whether he was missing something, or just going mad! Martin really hated getting into trouble, as did Jack, although people often assumed Jack didn't mind because of how regularly it happened. From a young age, teachers often seemed to get cross with him for doing things he didn't know how to not do, things that were part of his personality and so were hard for him to reign in. Sitting still and silently just did not feel natural and didn't make any sense to him. He did try to do it as much as he possibly could so that he wouldn't be told off too often. It was very uncomfortable to have to keep his muscles so tightly in check, and it made him feel like he was going to burst.

Also, it was the most natural thing in the world to say what he was thinking out loud, as soon as he thought it. Otherwise, he might lose the thought and he worried he would never remember it again. Besides, it was close to impossible for him to contain his impulses. He was very grateful that his mum had realised he really wasn't just being 'naughty' when he had to touch, hold, smell, and taste practically everything around him, as well as making noises unexpectedly. It was hard to understand why no-one else seemed to have caught on to the possibility that his mum, the woman he had lived with since birth, might know him better than anyone. Why did teachers assume that **they** knew Jack better than she did? Why did they think he was his 'normal self' and 'fine' in their company, these relative strangers who sometimes showed him little understanding and might immediately decide he was purposely interrupting them in class? Why did they take the natural behaviour of a four-, five-, six-, seven-, eight-, nine-, ten-year-old like a personal attack? Jack had learned to hide how he really felt about being in a chaotic, overwhelming classroom very early on. The months of crying and showing how unhappy and unable to cope he was when he started school in Reception had been met with teachers telling his mum "He's fine as soon as you leave" and them pulling him away from her in the mornings when he desperately clung to her arm. As his parents continued to insist that he had to go to school, it made Jack think this must just be normal and expected. The fact that teachers seemed so cross with his unhappiness made him think they must want him to hide it. He did everything he could to try to please them all.

Jack's mum and dad had talked about the problem being that teachers had lots of children they needed to try to understand, and all of them were different. They knew it was very hard for teachers to fit 'understand individual needs and adapt how I teach to meet the needs of each child' into their already too busy workload. Some teachers didn't even have a teaching assistant to support them, let alone any support or understanding from the lead staff.

Jack's mum had found online training about autism, ADHD, and so on, but maybe teachers didn't think of this, or didn't have the time or motivation to learn more about how they could understand the different needs of children in their classes. Maybe any training they did receive was very limited but they didn't realise a lot of useful information was missing. Jack's dad had said to his mum that the teachers were probably trying their best. Jack's mum had agreed, but also pointed out that the children were too.

It only feels like yesterday that Mr Brown told Mum "He's fine in school" *when I heard her trying to explain to him how unhappy I am and how exhausted I get.* At the time Jack had wanted to shout "Does 'fine' mean 'hates being here'!?" But as often happened, his real feelings got stuck in his throat.

But now, everything seemed so different. *This is getting weirder and weirder!*
Another strange thing was that it was nearly half an hour into the morning and Mr Brown hadn't set any work for them to sit quietly and get on with at their desks. Jack thought he needed to make sure he wasn't just imagining things or had somehow got really mixed up.
"Martin!" He quickly whispered.
"Just a minute." Martin replied, without lowering his voice or looking at Jack with his usual 'telling off' face he used when Jack talked to him in class.
"I just want to finish this chapter before Settling In Time finishes."
Settling In Time? What's that? Jack wondered to himself. He decided to not say anything else and just wait. He was still trying to process all the other differences. Although they were all very welcome changes to what he could remember school being and feeling like, it was a lot to make sense of.
"Okay. Finished. Now, what is it, you fruitloop?"
Well, this was more like it. Martin and Jack had known each other for so long that they had a relaxed familiarity with the way they spoke to one another. Jack's pet name for Martin was 'Martian'. Despite being good friends and very comfortable with each other, they were very different and found each other perplexing at times.
"What...what's going on?" Jack asked tentatively. Martin looked at him with a mixture

of surprise and amusement.
"Erm…we're sitting here in our classroom."
"Yes, I know. But who is that other teacher, there? And why are there only 8 of us? And how come we're allowed to sit where we want and, you know, be comfortable!?"
Martin laughed. "Who are you? What have you done with Jack?"
"Well, I thought I knew who I was when I woke up this morning, but since getting to school, everything seems sort of…different."
Martin looked at Jack, looked around the room, then back at Jack, shaking his head and laughing at his friend's silliness. Jack laughed back weakly and didn't have time to say anything else because just then Mr Brown stood up to speak.
"Okay, Thames Class, time to go to your first lesson, I'll see some of you this afternoon."
Now Jack was really confused. Mr Brown was still cheerful for one thing, and where on earth should he go for the first lesson? A couple of his classmates stayed in their seats. *Maybe they don't know what to do either,* Jack thought. But he felt it was safest to follow Martin as they usually had most of their classes together.
However, by the time Jack had left the classroom, there was no sign of Martin.
To his surprise, he saw a big fluffy Labrador curled up in a dog bed in the corridor just outside his classroom. The dog's head was flopped over the edge of her bed. Jack loved dogs, and after a moment's hesitation where he questioned whether it was safe to pet her, he

decided they wouldn't leave a dangerous dog unattended around children. He wondered if this must be the dog he had heard earlier.

"Hello," Jack said, crouching down to stroke the dog. As he did so, she rolled over onto her back and Jack was delighted to see how friendly she was.

"What's your name?" he asked the Labrador, trying to see the name on her tag as she frolicked about on her back.

"What do you mean 'what's your name', Jack?"

Just for a moment, he was extremely taken aback. Then the teacher, who had been watching them the whole time, went on.

"You know Violet."

Jack was rather relieved when he realised it was his art teacher talking, and not the dog.

Of course! It couldn't have been Violet speaking, what was I thinking? He didn't think that was a good thought to share out loud. He turned round and smiled at Mrs Miele.

"Where are you going, Jack?"

"I'm…I'm not completely sure which way to go."

Jack looked down and noticed Violet had walked over to a wall and was sniffing the display that was hung there, right by the words 'Where do you want to go?'. The words were surrounded by pictures of all sorts of different exciting activities. There was an artist at an easel, a cook chopping up vegetables, a chemist pouring brightly coloured liquids into beakers, a dancer mid-twirl wearing a shiny outfit, and about five more jobs illustrated. Jack was distracted by all the

possibilities the display was presenting.
"You like cooking, don't you Jack?" Mrs Miele spoke warmly and without any hint of hurrying him to answer her questions.
Jack was still trying to process the morning's strange, yet reassuring, events. Nothing was how it should be, except, everything was just how it ought to be. He usually felt so out of place, so overwhelmed and misunderstood at school. But, although things felt completely different, nothing, including himself (unusually), felt wrong.
"What do we like to say, Jack? 'It all depends on where you want to get to.'" Mrs Miele was tilting her head towards the wall display as she said this.

Now Jack really was having trouble computing this. Could it really be possible that the teachers didn't seem to mind what lesson he was in, as long as it was something he was interested in? Had he got that right? Jack had always been interested in food, both eating and cooking, and recently he had been thinking about how food is presented, and how people make it look so good. He had spent hours looking at how food is displayed online in adverts and also on the menus that came through his door at home. He was already quite good at cooking and baking, but he wasn't very confident about his creative skills.
I know you were still trying to decide between photography and art for this period, so you can

just try both of them for a bit longer if you haven't decided. Mr Brown is just about to start his photography lesson in your form room, and, as you know, I'm right next door in Derwent Class, if you want to come to my art class this time."

Mrs Miele gave Jack a while to make a decision. She simply continued stroking Violet so Jack didn't feel pressured.

"If it's okay, I think I'll do photography this time." He was still half expecting to be told he had got that wrong somehow. He hated the thought of upsetting teachers or making them cross, so spent most of his time at school being as careful as possible not to offend any of them. This usually meant going along with their suggestions or just answering "yes" when asked if everything was okay or if he had understood. He didn't dare tell them he definitely was not okay and hated being there, or that he hadn't followed any of what they had said because they'd said too much too quickly and hadn't written any of it down. It helped Jack to have reminders to look at and see what he was supposed to be doing, but the teachers were always in such a hurry to get through the lessons and to the next topic.

When they checked whether the children had understood before moving on to the next thing, Jack didn't feel he had the time or the courage to put up his hand and say "No, I need longer". Teachers didn't always really welcome this sort of honesty. It felt like the children who, like him, needed time to process things in a different way often got into trouble or left behind because the teachers assumed they just weren't paying attention or didn't want to learn.

But Mrs Miele just smiled and said "Sure, sure. I'm not offended," and wiped a fake tear from her eye with a playful wink. Jack smiled back and watched her go into her classroom as he walked back into Thames Room.

"Careful Jack!" Mr Brown exclaimed with his fingers half covering his eyes. "I was worried you were going to hit your head on the door frame. Remember to look at where you're going."
Now, Jack was thinking, this was more like the Mr Brown he knew, although he didn't actually sound cross.
"Sorry, sir." Jack said sheepishly.
"No harm done." Mr Brown responded with a soft smile. "You're okay, aren't you mate? I just know you need a bit of a reminder sometimes, like we all do. Being more mindful might seem new-fangled, but it's just common sense to be mindful of what you're doing, isn't it?"
"Yes, I guess so." Jack was reminded of what his mum often said to him about 'being in the moment' more, so that he didn't keep bashing himself on doors, chairs and tables, or dropping things.
Jack looked around the class and saw again that there were still just a few other children in the room. They all seemed to be working on different things on their own, and a couple of them were with one teacher or another. Unusually, Mr Brown wasn't bellowing from the front of the class while thirty children sat neatly in rows, taking notes and looking uncomfortable. In fact, Mr Brown was sitting down! He was at a table with two of Jack's classmates, smiling and chatting with them. *This is all very peculiar,* Jack thought. But at the same time, it made him feel at

ease to see everyone looking so relaxed and apparently happy to be there. That was always the strange thing about school as Jack remembered it, before everything got a bit topsy-turvy. He knew he hated being in school, but it often seemed to him that hardly anyone wanted to be there. And that included the teachers!
He regularly wondered what was the point of all these children and teachers spending every week day being cross and miserable.
It wasn't that Jack didn't enjoy learning. He loved it, in fact, and really wanted to learn lots of different things about the world. He simply couldn't see the point of a lot of the lessons in school. He wanted to know how everyday things worked, and how the subjects they were being taught were relevant to his life. There was always very little, if any, time spent explaining why the things they were learning would be useful to them one day. And saying something like "You never know when the Anglo-Saxon invasion will come up in conversation" made very little sense to a child whose main interests are computer games and having fun playing in parks with friends. Some teachers seemed bored of what they were teaching as well (probably because of being forced to teach for tests rather than having much scope for creativity). Or, if they were enthusiastic, only a few children in the class could ever benefit because there were just so many children, and always a few who weren't engaged, or were finding it hard to keep up, and just messed around. A single teacher, sometimes

with an additional support teacher, would naturally find it a struggle to keep the interest of a class of around 30 children with different needs. It would take an extraordinary teacher to keep up with this, day in, day out, especially when everything felt so rushed and chaotic.

Jack was often seen as one of those who messed around, and sometimes he probably did. After all, it was a very long time to have to sit still and keep quiet without breaks or water. Other times though, Jack became distracted by the noise of the more confident children in the class whispering because they already knew everything the teacher was saying, or had finished their work, or were simply bored. This would cause Jack to look around, which usually resulted in him being told off for not concentrating, but rarely the children who were better at getting round the teachers.

At times, Jack might not know what he was supposed to be doing because the one way the teacher had explained it just wasn't enough or suited to his way of learning. Instead of asking for another explanation, he did not want to look stupid or draw attention to himself, and so would fiddle with whatever was on his desk or rock on his chair. These things all helped him feel calmer and less anxious about not knowing what to do, but the teachers would tell him off for distracting others or not getting on with his work. *What work am I supposed to be getting on with!?* he would often be desperately wondering.

Now, in this classroom where he was used to feeling so overwhelmed and out of place, Jack found himself again feeling strangely calm. No-one was messing around, there were only seven children in the room including him, and the three teachers in the class were all smiling and being friendly with the children. It was as if everyone was happy to be there! The children were completely absorbed in what they were doing, and they were all doing their own thing. When Jack looked closer at a couple of the tables, he saw that one child was flicking through pictures on her phone, and another one was talking to a teaching assistant about zooming in to the mushroom she'd photographed and wanting to keep the image crisp. He realised that this was something he knew about, but wasn't sure if it was right to offer his assistance.

Just then, the teaching assistant looked round at Jack and waved for him to come over, announcing "Jack did that really well when he zoomed in on the Lego figure he was photographing."

Jack was really confused for a moment, but then remembered he had been setting up Lego figures in heroic poses and battle scenes at home. At the weekend, he had taken lots of photos of the figures on his phone.

"Ooh can I see?" his classmate, Ava, asked him.

"Sure." Jack replied, a little bemused and unsure whether the teacher was about to tell him to put his phone away. But she didn't. The teaching assistant, Miss Taylor, actually turned round the free chair next to her invitingly for Jack to sit on. Jack could not remember feeling so good, so wanted, in school before. He strode over to their table, and held his phone down so that Ava and Miss Taylor could see the screen, scrolling through his photos of Lego figures until he found an example of how he had zoomed in and managed to make the image clear and crisp. He showed them the different settings that can be accessed on his phone, and helped Ava find them on hers.

"Thanks, Jack," Ava said, "It's actually really easy now you've shown me!"

Jack smiled and for a moment wasn't sure whether to stay there next to Ava and Miss Taylor or go back to his seat. There were some free chairs because of how few children there were in this class, so he guessed it didn't really matter which chair he sat on. Just as he had this thought, Jack spotted a padded, black, swivel chair that no-one was sitting on.
"Would it be okay if I use that chair, Miss?" Jack was getting used to the idea that the teachers were a lot more friendly and relaxed at the moment, so felt braver than usual to ask a question.
"Yes, of course! As long as no-one else is using it, you can sit on any chair you like."
"Brilliant." *What a luxury!* Jack thought to himself, he really couldn't believe his luck. How funny to be so delighted by a comfortable chair, but Jack really came alive when his senses were positively stimulated. He took the few steps over to where this throne of a chair was situated, and sunk into it with great satisfaction. The padded seat and back were so much more comfortable than the usual plastic school chairs, and this one even spun around and could be lowered up and down. Jack was quite tall, so he raised the seat up a couple of inches.
"This is so much better than being scrunched up in my usual chair!" Jack told Mr Brown, who had just walked close by. Mr Brown laughed and said "Yes, I must admit it usually does look like you're stretching out like a telescope when you stand up!"

Jack chuckled and imagined himself sitting down with all his limbs pulled in tightly and then standing up and unfolding in slow motion. Suddenly, that gave him an idea for a stop-motion video he could film later with his Lego figures.
"What would you like your next project to be about, Jack?" Mr Brown then asked.
"Well, what you just said made me think of doing a video with my Lego figures so that they start small and then stretch out bigger and bigger like, well, a telescope opening up, like you said." Jack had no idea if this was the sort of thing Mr Brown meant when he asked about his next project, but he was feeling so confident that he guessed, even if he did get it all wrong, the teachers weren't going to tell him off anyway.
"I like your thinking, Jack. But maybe we can come up with something similar that you could photograph rather than video, to get the stretching out effect. Maybe using weird angles or shadows?"
Jack felt a little pang of nerves…excitement maybe…in his stomach as Mr Brown was talking. It wasn't like the wriggling caterpillars from the mornings before going to school, but more like butterfly wings fluttering around. It was such an unusual feeling to be reassured in this way by a teacher. He felt so enthusiastic about finding interesting ways to take photos. Although he really didn't want to get out of his comfy chair, he went over to the box of scrap paper and grabbed a pencil from the pot next to that so he

could do some sketches for ideas of how he could set up the photos. While he sketched, he swung his legs side to side so that his chair turned left and right with the momentum. This helped him stay focused and engaged with his chosen assignment. It was a little bit miraculous – he'd been in school for ages and no-one had told him something he'd done was wrong! The little flutter returned to his stomach when he realised this. Was this what it felt like to be actually happy in school!?

But maybe I shouldn't get too used to this. Jack thought to himself. *After all, this is such a new feeling and as it's not one I've felt before, there's every possibility the usual sense of dreading school and all the teachers being unhappy will return. The uniform alone…* And just then, Jack looked down at what he was wearing and saw that he wasn't actually wearing the navy, stiff school uniform at all! His clothes were indeed navy, but he was wearing the comfortable tracksuit his mum had finally found after months of searching for something he found soft enough and tolerable to wear. He then looked around and saw that all of his classmates and his teachers were wearing comfortable clothes as well. *No wonder the teachers are in such a good mood,* he thought, *this is more like how they are on dress-down days.* Jack had often felt that every day should be a dress-down day, everyone always seemed so much more relaxed on those non-uniform days.

Mr Brown looked from the clock to his watch and back at the clock again.

"Miss Taylor, is that the right time?"
"Oh dear! Yes, it is, I'm afraid we're going to be late for lunch!"
Being late for lunch was not good news for Jack at all. In the first place, he loved food and eating, and secondly, he really did not like standing in a long queue. He wasn't sure whether it was more to do with the seemingly endless time he was standing there, the fact that other people were standing in his personal space, or the sheer chaotic mess of how his senses felt while queuing.
"Oh dear I am sorry, class. Shall we go and join the queue? Hopefully Mrs Miele's class are late as well so we can get in there first and there won't be too long to wait!"
Jack walked to the dinner hall with his classmates and teachers (which was new because usually the teachers went off to some mystery venue at lunch times - which he assumed was probably just the staff room, but who knows?). When they got there, just a few children and a couple of teachers were already in the line waiting for their lunch.
"Great," Mr Brown said to Jack and the other few children from the photography class, "Mrs Miele's class **is** late too, and so we won't have to wait very long."
He looked at Jack and smiled, almost like he was reading Jack's anxious thoughts about queuing. Then Jack noticed that there were fewer tables in the lunch hall than he remembered, and the ones that were there were more spread out, just like

the classroom tables. The tables were also smaller, and didn't have as many seats around them.

****

It wasn't long before Jack was near the front of the queue. He watched what the people who were already getting their lunch were doing so as not to get it wrong when it was his turn. He could see that the cooks and food servers looked just as happy and relaxed as everyone else today. This was the least unusual thing about the day. Maybe it was because of how much Jack enjoyed food, but he was often more relaxed at lunch times, especially once he had his food and was out of the queue.
"Hi, Jack! What do you fancy today?" The kitchen supervisor was always friendly, but he couldn't remember her knowing his name before. He realised all the teachers he had seen that day had known his name, and they had all smiled at him warmly when they passed.
"This is the veggie lasagne and that one there is the meat one. And there are also the usual jacket potatoes and fillings over there, and make sure you help yourself to the salad bits, my love."
"Meat one." came Jack's response. He wanted to say 'please', and meant to be polite, but it just did not come out, or if it did, the words came out as a whisper and no-one heard. People always put

pressure on him to say 'please' and 'thank you'. Sometimes they prompted him just when he was about to say it - the pressure of which made him unable to say anything else. Other times, he already had said 'please' or 'thank you' so quietly that people just didn't hear.
There were lots of times when Jack simply could not say the words he wanted to say. It had been that way for as long as he could remember. It felt like the words got stuck. Usually, this made Jack feel terrible, but the supervisor just smiled and said "No problem, lovey." and all Jack felt was relief.

A Dream Day at School

So far, every experience that day since he sat at his desk in the morning really had felt like a huge weight had been lifted from Jack's shoulders. He could feel his muscles relaxing, his spirit lifting. It was a strange day, but he felt happier than he had felt for a long time.

As Jack walked away from the food counter with his tray, he noticed some children were walking out of the dinner room with their trays of food.

"Hi, Jack. Are you going to eat in our form room again today? I might stay here because Izzy wants to tell me something." Jack's friend Imani had bounded over to greet him with a beaming smile. Jack wondered if maybe he had been standing there looking unsure of where to go, and this might be why Imani had come over. They were quite good friends, but Imani didn't always want to talk much. Jack knew this was normal for him, and usually Imani would just give him a smile and nod when they passed each other.

"Oh, yeah I think I will go to the form room." Jack waited a moment for Imani's response, partly to check whether he had heard right and it actually was okay to go to his classroom with his food.

"Okay then, see you later!" Imani said cheerily waving as he walked over to where Izzy was sitting.

Wow, I think that's more than he's said to me all year! He seems more confident. I wonder if he's feeling more relaxed too.

When Jack got to his classroom, he found Mr Brown playing a game on his laptop. Next to him was a plate with a half-eaten jacket potato that he was taking forkfuls of every now and then. Looking up towards Jack as he walked through the door, Mr Brown smiled with cheeks bulging with the latest mouthful. Jack was still a bit unsure about this relaxed lunchtime arrangement. There were four other children in the room, one of whom wasn't even from his own form. They were all doing their own thing, some cheerfully chatting and some quietly listening or reading a book, all while eating their lunches. Jack tentatively went to his desk and sat down. He still had the fiddle toys lined up on the edge of his desk that he had taken from the box earlier that morning. He looked around and saw that other children had some fiddle toys on their desks too.

****

Time seemed to pass in a flash. Thoughts about the strange but wonderful day sailed through Jack's mind.
He must have been daydreaming while he was processing his morning and enjoying his food, because the next thing he knew, Mr Brown was saying "Oops, five minutes until next lesson.

We'd best take our trays back to the canteen and put our rubbish in the bins."
The way he simply declared that this was something they all needed to do, including him, the teacher, rather than ordering them to do it quickly, really helped Jack feel less pressured to get it done before someone told him off. Jack didn't know why it seemed so much easier to get on with this task than it might usually feel, but he just got on and did it with everyone else quite happily.
This day is like a dream! Jack thought while smiling to himself. It was already half way through the day, and he really wasn't sure what subject he had next, but Jack felt excited about whatever was to come.
Imani came over to him again once Jack had put his tray and rubbish away where he had seen others putting theirs.
"I think it's basketball again this afternoon." he said to Jack with that beaming smile again. "Are you going straight there now? I'll come with you if you are."
"Err, yeah. Okay." Jack thought this would be a good way to make sure he ended up going in the direction he needed to actually go, so he let Imani exit the door before him. Imani was quite animated and was telling Jack what their friend Izzy had said to him at lunch time. Jack didn't catch all of it because Imani kept stepping on the posts and steps that they passed, and between that was spinning and jumping off things. Jack worked out that it was something to do with the

books they were both reading and really into. Jack usually read comics instead of books. He loved English and enjoyed creative writing, but was just really enjoying comics at the moment. Since he was very young, he had loved flicking through books looking at the illustrations. Jack often told his mum that he had now read "936 out of 1260", or whatever he was up to now, of the series he was currently reading.

It didn't usually feel like he should tell people in school about what he was currently obsessed with, but today everything felt easy and that he was more accepted. Jack matched Imani's bouncy energy and told him about how many comics he had read and what he loved about them.

"Brilliant!" Imani exclaimed, seeming genuinely delighted for his friend.

Jack followed Imani over to the other three children and the two teachers on the basketball court. As the teacher began the class, Jack realised that this must be everyone who was doing PE together. He smiled to himself, feeling still ever more growing relief that there wasn't going to be the usual chaotic, noisy scramble of children around him. In fact, it was so relaxed that the teacher asked them all what they wanted to do in the lesson. The common consensus was that they wanted to start by taking turns trying to get the balls in the basket. It was such a fun lesson! They were all running around after their balls once they'd tried to score, and Jack was thoroughly worn out by the time the lesson was over.

He walked with Imani and Martin back towards their form room, tired but content. The other two boys had jumped up onto the low wall that surrounded a raised bed of herbs in the courtyard in front of their class.
As Jack went to do the same, his foot slipped and…

****

"Jack. Jaaack!" Martin was nudging Jack in the ribs with his elbow, trying to shout-whisper to get him to wake up. Jack was startled and sat bolt upright in his chair, where he found he was sat at his desk in his crowded classroom. Mr Brown was booming instructions across the class, and Martin looked very worried that Jack was going to get into trouble for falling asleep at his desk.
Jack looked around. A crowded classroom with all 28 students crammed around desks.
Everyone, including him, was wearing the same stiff uniform.
"Jack, turn round and face the front!" Jack's shoulders stiffened, he could feel panic rising and felt like he might cry. *It was just a dream,* he thought to himself.

I can't do this anymore!

And that was the last day Jack was able to force himself into this school.

Afterward – notes from the author

The end of Jack's story may have made you sad, and maybe even cry. It was very hard to write and every time I've re-read it I have cried. It might not be a bad thing if it did upset you.
If you're a parent and reading this made you cry, maybe it resonates with you and I want to tell you that you're not alone. If you're experiencing this now, there is a light at the end of the tunnel.
If you're a teacher and you find this upsetting, it's probably because you have the compassion to know that you have children in your classes who will be experiencing these feelings, and parents who are desperately trying to get you to understand.
Although this is, obviously, a fictional story, every one of the problems faced by Jack and his family have come from the direct experiences of my younger son, Jobi, during his time at three mainstream schools. It took me (with support from my husband) until our son was 12 years old to begin to feel as though my fight for appropriate understanding, education and support was actually getting somewhere. And when he was 14, for the first time ever, he started attending a school that meets his needs completely, and he is now a very different boy. He has just turned 15 years old, and is now more confident, has a sense of who he is, and LOVES going to school.

Our journey to help Jobi feel less anxious and unhappy was a long one. From the beginning, I tried my hardest to find ways to encourage him to go into school, or even to just come out of his bedroom, but nothing worked. I called the school each morning for the first week or so, and then emailed every morning for weeks, to explain that he was just too anxious to come in, or do anything else. Jobi was completely burned out, and it was another new way of approaching parenting that we had to get our heads round. It was hard for family members to understand, including his brother, who has never had any problems going into school because the imposed structure works really well for him. I learned more about what Jobi was going through now that from appearances he was struggling with the most basic tasks. We'd already had experience of Jobi trying to find a way to feel more in control of things and less anxious when he developed difficulties around eating and a fear of being sick. This time, even being as gentle and accommodating as we could with him was still resulting in extreme nervous system responses. Having some sense of control over what is going on around them is essential for people with PDA, so that their nervous system isn't triggered into a state of fight/flight/freeze/fawn/ flop. These are all instinctive survival responses that are activated subconsciously.

Fight can look like answering back, lashing out, anger, noticeable frustration.

Flight looks like running or walking away.

Freeze can appear as submissiveness or withdrawing. The individual is rigid, not talking, and tense.
Fawn means trying to make other people like you, or make them laugh.
And flop looks similar to freeze, except the individual goes 'floppy' instead of tensing up.
Jobi's experiences in mainstream school had led to his nervous system being burned out from the daily assault to his senses and lack of autonomy. It was going to take time, patience, and understanding to help him recover. Demand avoidance and the ever-present anxiety that accompanies it has been tricky to navigate and has required a lot of patience, love, and acceptance. It's been an absolute voyage of self-discovery for all of us, but especially for Jobi.

It was hard to know what life would be like for Jobi after everything had fallen apart. His dad and I didn't know if he would ever leave the house again. There is still some work to do to help Jobi feel confident enough to go to new places with people he doesn't know. He will get there when he is ready, with support.

School and Mental Health

For most of Jobi's time in school I had asked to pursue an Education and Health Care Plan assessment (this is a legal document that should ensure that children who require extra support and understanding, receive it.) However, until Jobi got to the point of not being able to attend school, primary school SENDCos (Special Educational Needs and Disabilities Coordinators) had always put me off. They'd say it was too difficult or time consuming, or that Jobi didn't meet the criteria. Like many other children, Jobi's mental health plummeted during COVID, but even when I reported the severe difficulties he was experiencing to his primary school, there continued to be a distinct lack of support. I couldn't help thinking when we got to the point when he was no longer able to go into school at all, that maybe we should have ignored teachers years ago and just stuck to our guns and done what we knew was best for Jobi.
It was hard not to feel guilty, but we had trusted that his teachers had his best interests at heart. It took a long time for it to sink in that costs were the priority in these financially struggling schools.

Teachers often have certain methods they use, or told to use, when children stop going into school. In our case, some were more sensitive than others. We knew from the reports of Jobi's former classmates that some teachers really didn't get it at all. It's sad to think that our family was more fortunate than many across the country in a similar situation. For instance, there happened to be a SENDCo at Jobi's school who had some understanding of PDA. They could translate Jobi's difficulties and behaviour to his teachers (because the same information coming from me hadn't been enough). It was clear from the limitations of the strategies used to try to rebuild Jobi's trust and feeling of safety in the school that it is next to impossible for mainstream schools to meet the needs of children who are overwhelmed by chaotic environments, without thinking outside the box.

Other professionals got involved after a while when Jobi hadn't been receiving any education at all for weeks. The attendance officer was quite understanding when I explained that the problem wasn't that he didn't want to learn, and indeed had found things online that he was interested to learn about. They still didn't know what to suggest.

Some parents in similar situations are told to take away devices and make home boring. I don't remember such uncaring suggestions being given to us. When a child is already struggling, home is often the only place where they feel safe, understood, and loved. The idea that making this one safe environment as stressful as everywhere else is hard to comprehend. Overstretched and underpaid teachers and professionals

undoubtedly want to be able to do more to support struggling children but the pressure of making going to school look good often outweighs everything else. The mainstream education system can feel like a place where it's more important to get a box ticked than to ensure children are secure and happy.
If a child or young person experiences anxiety due to attending school, they may become withdrawn from their normal daily life and exhibit changes in their behaviour. They may find it hard to get out of bed, clean themselves and get dressed. They might have a social phobia, like agoraphobia, and find it difficult to leave the house or go to any social activities. If their anxiety is misunderstood by teachers, professionals, or parents, the child or young person may suffer further mental health difficulties due to not being supported and feeling misunderstood. They might feel there is something wrong with them and harm themselves physically.

Many children who are struggling in school are being shouted at or treated unkindly in other ways and told they should just be more resilient when it creates anxiety. It's close to impossible for a child to learn resilience in an environment they find traumatic.

Post-traumatic stress disorder (PTSD) is triggered by traumatic events in a person's life. This can include bullying, abuse, witnessing or being subjected to something distressing, and also being in an environment where you feel unsafe or overwhelmed, or many other difficult experiences. The mainstream school environment traumatises children like Jobi because of the lack of autonomy, constant high demands and chaotic sensory elements. PDA can be regarded as a nervous system disability because the nervous system is constantly on high alert. If a child or young person suffers from long term stress and anxiety, because of a school not understanding or meeting their additional needs for example, they can develop depression and behavioural challenges. A child displaying challenging behaviour is often unable to regulate their emotions and reacts out of stress and anxiety to what they're asked to do. Some children, especially those who are neurodivergent (and particularly PDA), haven't yet developed impulse control due to underlying difficulties with executive functioning. This can lead to mental health problems because of the resulting low self- esteem from being constantly corrected (both internal and external).

There is woefully little support for families in a similar situation to ours. Adequate and authentic support is in short supply. Getting support or even being taken seriously is a complete lottery. Whenever I sought help, often none was given, but for reasons only known to the people doing the assessments, other families around us were given plans and support workers. Both my sons have had a hard time in mainstream schools. At times, my sons were blamed for being bullied. "If only he wasn't so quirky" and other appallingly toxic views from teachers have done lasting damage to my sons' capacity to trust others and see them as inherently good and trustworthy. Some of the professionals we ended up enlisting to help our sons were also unwilling or unable to look beyond their assumptions and judgements. Change needs to start from the top, with the attitude of the people in charge of the care of our children. It took us a long time to find people who could see beyond their assumptions about why Jobi was so unhappy in school, and use their more well-informed knowledge of sensory differences and neurodiversity to help him. It wasn't until the very long process of requesting and then receiving an EHCP for Jobi that we began receiving funded support.

Many of the improvements that help Jack feel more relaxed and comfortable to be himself within the Dream School are present in Jobi's new school. It's full of happy teachers and other staff who don't get cross with the children - that is, if they do, there isn't any shouting nor detentions given out. Instead, there is a collaborative and friendly approach. Jobi is thriving, and delights in telling me what he has done at school most days as soon as he gets home.

I'm a firm believer that everyone is trying their best, children and adults included. I also believe this is directly influenced by whether our nervous system is in a state of regulation or not. Smaller class sizes, relaxed clothing and atmosphere, access to what the child needs (fiddle toys, etc.) whenever regulation is necessary, and interest-led learning are all dreams for a lot of parents of children who struggle in school. They are also big asks for most mainstream schools due to funding cuts and outdated systems. But, what if more time and money was put into investing and looking at evidence for making school – such an important part of every person's life – a place where everyone wants to be in the first place and actually thrives?

So, my message is that 'dream school' is not impossible. I know that because it's our current lived experience. Motivated and well-informed teachers, a less stressful and chaotic environment, and genuinely supported children is not an impossible, unattainable dream for children in mainstream schools. We parents should not be made to feel like we are doing something wrong by trying to get our neurodivergent and/or anxious children the education and support they are entitled to so they can have the same chances as everyone else.

I also feel that the traumatic events of the recent global pandemic and the effects that has had on us all, but most importantly babies, toddlers, children and teens, is often neglected when considering the care and mental health services available. Young peoples' views of the world will inevitably have been partly shaped by what we all went through. Maybe the privileged position of the people who run our countries removes them from having any insight into COVID-19's long term effects on the majority of the population. But I remember what it was like. Jobi does too. He remembers he thought he was going to die.

Very little has been learned from the fact that when COVID prevented children from going into school, many who had **always** struggled to go in actually thrived at home or with alternative ways to learn. It's been understood for years that different people learn in many different ways. There are lots more creative and inclusive options to enable the children who don't fit into the hectic classroom environment of mainstream schools to also thrive. Most people undoubtedly go into teaching with the intention of helping children to learn and develop into happy well-adjusted individuals. The mainstream system, however, isn't set up to enable this to be possible for all children. There isn't much room for responding to individual needs because the emphasis in most schools is on obedience and academic attainment. There are, however, many adaptations that can help autistic children, especially those with high anxiety and demand

avoidance, to feel better understood and accepted. These adaptations work for all children, because there will be many children who aren't neurodivergent who also feel overwhelmed and unhappy in the current school conditions. When children feel better, they are more likely to be calmer and able to cope with what is expected of them.
Children are not meant to be miserable in school. Why has this been normalised?

"The system of schooling we call 'conventional' was not founded on a scientific understanding of how children learn. It was actually developed initially, quite explicitly, for the purpose of obedience training and indoctrination. It was invented at a time when people believed that children are naturally sinful and must be strictly trained to obey authority in order to overcome that sinfulness."
From 'Changing Our Minds' by Naomi Fisher.

I know from experience that there are hundreds of parents whose only option has been to give up their jobs to home educate their children because, despite their desperate efforts to get appropriate help for their children in school, there is not adequate support, funding or understanding available. It is truly disgraceful how much extra stress parents of children with additional needs are put through. There isn't sufficient accountability with the local authorities who are meant to be ensuring everything is in place for children who are most anxious and in need of support. It's the children (and their parents) who are most often blamed (and fined) when they're not able to force themselves to go into school anymore, despite the reason for this being that their needs are not being met.

There are thousands of children in this country who want to go to school, and parents who've tried everything they can to get them in, but it's just not safe for them and damaging to their mental health to be in the chaotic, overpopulated environment.

Teachers need better wages, more funding and support so they can look after struggling children - and all children - properly. They do an essential job, but aren't treated as such.

A Personal Note

As a side note, we are often told that it's the female presentation of autism or PDA that includes masking and social anxiety, but I feel this is very misleading. I believe these are simply more recently understood and accepted possible parts of any autistic person's way of being in the world. It doesn't help that autistic girls and women have been disproportionately undiagnosed for years, but as is often the case in science and psychology, this is, I believe, more likely due to the fact that males were the focus of original studies and taken as the norm. Normalised masculine presentations were written into the diagnostic criteria, but masking wasn't considered because it isn't something males are socially expected to have to do. It is more of a social norm for females to people-please, smile, and be of service to others, so it is no wonder that girls and women's masking has been more obvious and commonplace. However, boys and men do mask too, especially now that it is more socially accepted for males to show their softer (feminine) side. Masking occurs when neurodivergent people feel uncomfortable with the people they are with or the situation they are in.

Something that started making it easier for me to parent a child with PDA autism was when I realised that I was once a PDA child. I also felt lost and like I desperately needed to feel in

control of my life. I couldn't stand pressure, and felt it deeply everywhere.
As a girl I had the societal pressures to please everyone, smile and look attractive. I never felt attractive (partly thanks to a lot of name-calling from boys my age). But I was good at the people pleasing role. My burn-out didn't occur until my late teens and into my early 20s. This is when I realised something needed to change, and I began to learn how to reset my nervous system.
There are many relaxation methods, including qi gong and meditation which I've been using and teaching for over 20 years, that help neurodivergent people to feel less overwhelmed and more connected with themselves and the outer universe. These methods work for everyone, all people struggle with anxiety and stress after all. I'd love these simple practices to be more commonplace so that children know there are ways to help themselves feel better.

Advice for Teachers from an Occupational Therapist

Not surprisingly, school can be a challenging environment for individuals with PDA, although the hardest part for some can be just waking up and getting into school! All autistic people can struggle if the environment isn't right, and PDA is no exception. If you are at school or college it is good to be clear about what helps or doesn't help. And if you are not able to be in school, well you are not alone.

In a typical school day the level of demands on learners can feel overwhelming. As an Occupational Therapist I am often asked by parents and schools to advise on sensory needs or PDA specifically. My expertise comes from years of studying classroom dynamics, but the real experts are always the children and their families. Each individual is different, and I often find that parents know far better than I do about the best strategies to use with their child.

That said, there are a few starting points I can give teachers to help them make things go a little more smoothly both in and out of the classroom on any given day.

*Be fair and consistent and be prepared to defend your fairness. They need to know that what you expect today is what you'll expect tomorrow.

And that there is equity in the rewards or sanctions given to them and the wider class.

*Show respect, and be willing to apologise, even when it isn't your fault. If a learner is upset with you, they are unlikely to work for you. Fixing that relationship is important. Starting the conversation with, 'I'm sorry I upset you, that wasn't my intention.' is a great start to putting things right and makes learners much more receptive to continuing the conversation. Show your learners you like them unconditionally. Some young people have challenging behaviours. Try to show them that although you may not like some of their behaviour, you do like and respect them as an individual.

*It's a partnership, sometimes it helps to meet the learner halfway by 'throwing away the rulebook' about adults asserting authority and children obeying. Use reward systems with caution as these can cause added pressure. All or nothing systems do not work well for most learners with PDA. So, for example, instead of saying if you have a good week, you can have a reward, use a token board system where learners get their reward after completing so many good lessons. This way nothing is lost if things go wrong as tokens which have been earned can be carried over to the next week. It's also much harder for a learner to sabotage their own success for fear of failure, as progressive reward systems mean that it's very hard to fail.

*Build in flexibility and choices to your day and allow processing time. It's a fine balance between giving options and making those options overwhelming. I usually suggest giving two options, when it comes to tasks and to make those options open to the whole class. Then negotiate further with individuals if needed. It might take a learner a while to process or come on board with the activity so respect and give this time. The key is to keep in mind your objective rather than your lesson or plan. If your aim is to improve writing, and your learner is happy to write, does it really matter what they write about? Does it matter whether they do Maths before English? If they complete the tasks.

*Think carefully about change. How can you make it a preferred change? When is the best time to tell the learner about that change? What contingency plans do you have in place if the change doesn't work? A change that is planned for is rarely as devastating as one that isn't.

*Use of indirect language is very helpful when getting the best from the individual, framing instructions in a way that enables the learner such as "I wonder if we can..."; "Maybe we could investigate..." or "Let's see if we can make something..."

*Use of humour and distraction can be a handy way to temporarily press 'pause' and ease the child's anxiety and support processing time.

*Get to know the special interests of your learners. Watch videos, read books and understand that interest as well as you can. It is your most valuable tool. Talking about it will help calm them when they are upset and engage them in their work. For learners who are struggling, developing individualised schemes of work or projects around their special interest will make an enormous difference. For some children using characters of interest can help depersonalise demands, as you are not personally asking them to do something. Try to find a character voice you can use to make requests, or you could find a toy or puppet to represent the character. This can take a bit of practice, but drama and role play appeal to many children with PDA. You can also use the child's momentary actions or focus to transition them into an activity; for example, if a child is drawing a knight, you could sketch a little picture at the top of the worksheet you'd like the child to do, saying 'Look, your knight is here to watch you do this and then we can finish your big picture'. There is very little, that with a little forethought cannot be done this way. Trust me, it is worth the effort.

*Ensure sensory needs are met, for those with sensory processing needs, understanding what their presentation looks like when over or under stimulated is really important to be able to offer them strategies or options in the moment before they are already too overstimulated, and the demand will seem too much. Having a sensory profile or a sensory diet, usually informed by an OT is vital for knowing what is the right sensory strategy or opportunity to offer. More specific and individual pieces of work such as a sensory ladder, or the interoception curriculum (Maher) are really valuable in understanding the experiences of the individual and supporting them to understand themselves and advocate for what they need. Many learners are very insightful to their own sensory needs, whether they fully understand why or not. Listening to their experiences and preferences is paramount. Opportunity to retreat to a quiet or sensory rich environment as appropriate, and a way to indicate they need time out without needing to seek permission is what will help them get through the day. The more these things are normalised and modelled by staff and those around them, the easier they are for the learner to use without fear of being different or being singled out. I much prefer to see a classroom that has options for seating, fiddle tools which are freely accessible, and movement opportunities for all, treating all learners as individuals.

*Try whenever possible to avoid sending learners home because you feel that their behaviour has become unmanageable. If you do so it is likely to quickly become a negative cycle and break the trust. Work with parents to find other strategies

to help the learner to calm down in school. Tune in to the anxiety and panic which underlies the child's behaviour, we don't chastise children who are having panic attacks, we support them to calm down.
Working with parents and relevant professionals to find out what works best for the individual and support collaborative approaches to learning is the key to creating a successful environment.

*Above all remember that you won't get it right all of the time. What's important is that when it does go wrong, you analyse why and make changes so that the next day is a better one. Work with parents, be honest with them always. Together you will get there.

Alison Harrod
Specialist Occupational Therapist
Bursting with Potential

Acknowledgements

For any parents wondering which way to turn for support, I would like to highlight a number of very good and supportive resources which provide invaluable information on Facebook (a haven for parents with nowhere else to turn). In particular, Dr Naomi Fisher (whose books are a go-to for many parents in our situation); Casey Ehrlich, Ph.D. from At Peace Parents (truly wonderful advice for PDA parenting); and the PDA Society Facebook page, as well as their website. There are many other helpful pages and people. I have received the most amazing support through my local area SEND support page, and from individuals who have provided succinct information regarding EHCP assessments, etc., which is so hard to find amongst the dizzying complexity of the processes involved in getting support for the children who need it most. We wouldn't have made it through the EHCP process without the support of Julie Scott, thank you (again!). The first place I found support was with Pinpoint Cambridgeshire. This is an organization run by parent carers to help other parent carers find support, and to learn how they can have a voice in the future of their children.
The organization that helped Jobi to recover from school burn out, and be able to trust an education setting again, was Red Balloon of the Air, Cambridge. I want to give them a huge thank you to for the invaluable part they played in

getting our son to the point where he felt accepted again.
I would also like to thank Chip Colquhoun for his confidence building and fun sessions with Jobi, and Alison Harrod for seeing, from the beginning, that our bright boy just needed appropriate support and understanding to help him shine.
I'm a strong, independent woman (who very likely also has PDA), and I am very much aware that I'm the catalyst for ensuring Jobi's and his older brother, Mani's, wellbeing. However, I couldn't have asked for a more considerate, loving, and supportive partner than my husband, Joe. Thank you forever.

For the myriad life lessons I've learned over the years, many thanks to my family, a lot of whom are no longer here. Thank you to my friends who have listened to me over the years, I love you all very much.
I would like to dedicate this book in part to my Mum, who was always a most loving and generous influence on my sons. I'm so sorry she didn't get to see the boys become teenagers, but she will always be in our hearts.

Printed in Great Britain
by Amazon

43157894R10046